JF
Gelsey,
Scooby-D
Horror

D0392897

Hoopster Horror

Written by
James Gelsey

Scooby-Doo! and the hoopster h

JF Gelsey   58787

Gelsey, James.
Goodland Public Library

A
LITTLE APPLE
PAPERBACK

SCHOLASTIC INC.

New York   Toronto   London   Auckland   Sydney
Mexico City   New Delhi   Hong Kong   Buenos Aires

If you purchased this book without a cover, you should be aware that this book is stolen property. It was reported as "unsold and destroyed" to the publisher, and neither the author nor the publisher has received any payment for this "stripped book."

No part of this publication may be reproduced in whole or in part, or stored in a retrieval system, or transmitted in any form or by any means, electronic, mechanical, photocopying, recording, or otherwise, without written permission of the publisher. For information regarding permission, write to Scholastic Inc., Attention: Permissions Department, 557 Broadway, New York, NY 10012.

ISBN 0-439-54606-0

Copyright © 2005 by Hanna-Barbera.
SCOOBY-DOO and all related characters and elements
are trademarks of and © Hanna-Barbera.
CARTOON NETWORK and logo are trademarks of and
© Cartoon Network.
(s05)
Published by Scholastic Inc. All rights reserved.
SCHOLASTIC, LITTLE APPLE, and associated logos are
trademarks and/or registered trademarks of Scholastic Inc.

12 11 10 9 8 7 6 5 4 3 2 1   5 6 7 8 9/0

Special thanks to Duendes del Sur for cover and interior illustrations.
Printed in the U.S.A.
First printing, March 2005

Chapter 1

As the Mystery Machine cruised down the road, a melody filled the van as Shaggy sang,

"Denny the Dragon lived in a shack
Down by the beach with sand
on his back. . . ."

Scooby did a little jig as Shaggy continued.

"He played in the sun and swam in the sea,
Having lots of fun with you and me. . . ."

Up front, Daphne bopped her head along to the music. Fred thumped the steering wheel like a drum, and Velma quietly tapped her foot.

"Jeepers, I haven't heard anyone sing

1

GOODLAND PUBLIC LIBRARY
GOODLAND, KANSAS 67735

'Denny the Dragon' since I was little," Daphne said.

"Sure brings me back," Fred added. "I used to watch his show all the time when I was a kid."

Shaggy and Scooby popped their heads up front.

"And now the big finish," Shaggy cried out.

Everyone joined in as Shaggy sang, ". . . *cause Denny loves you, tooooooo!*"

"That was fun!" Daphne laughed.

"I must admit," Velma said, "it certainly is a feel-good kind of song."

"Just trying to get everyone into the spirit of things," Shaggy said. "Like, it's not every day you get to visit your favorite dragon's home."

Daphne looked puzzled.

"What are you talking about, Shaggy?" she asked.

"We're going to visit Denny's cave," Shaggy replied. He realized that no one was laughing any- more. "Like, aren't we?"

Velma shook her head. "Shaggy, we're going to visit the Dragons' Cave, all right, but that's not Denny's home."

"Rit's not?" asked Scooby. "Roo rives there?"

"No one lives there, Scooby," Fred said. "It's the name of the new basketball arena. It's where the Dragons play."

"We're going to watch dragons play bas- ketball?" Shaggy gasped. He turned to Scooby. "Man, how cool is that, Scoob?"

"Rit's Scooby cool!" he barked.

"So, like, how do they dribble and stuff?" Shaggy wondered. He and Scooby tried to picture a team of dragons playing basketball.

"Listen, you two," Velma interrupted. "Dragons don't play basketball."

Shaggy nodded. "I guess it would be hard," he said. "I'll bet football's their game."

Daphne shook her head in disbelief. "Shaggy, dragons don't play football, either," she said. "They're not real."

Shaggy's eyes widened in surprise as he looked out the window. "Dragons aren't real, huh?" he asked. "Then what's that?"

As the van turned into a parking lot, it passed an enormous inflatable dragon blowing smoke from its nostrils. It stood nearly three stories high.

"ROOOOOAAAAAARRRR!" cried the monster.

"Rikes!" Scooby cried as he dove under the seat.

"Relax, Scooby, that's just Fireball, the

team mascot," Fred said.

As the van drove on, Shaggy kept one eye on the dragon. "So tell me again why we're visiting a dragon's cave  that's not really a cave and has no real dragons in it?" he asked.

Daphne turned around in her seat. "Because we have passes to visit the team's practice facility," she said. "We won them at the charity bazaar last month, remember?"

Shaggy nodded as the van pulled up to a security gate. Fred rolled down his window.

"You kids sure you're in the right place?" asked the security guard.

Fred handed the passes to the guard.

"Okay, then," the guard said, tipping his hat. "Take this entry permit with you. Put half on the dashboard and carry the other half with you. Park over there and go in through the green door."

Fred parked the van right next to a stretch limousine.

"Jinkies! Look at the size of that car," Velma exclaimed. "That must belong to Wings Monroe."

"The star basketball player?" Daphne asked.

"Yeah, it's, like, the only car big enough to hold him if he wants to stretch out for a nap," Shaggy joked.

"I don't think it's his," Velma said. "Unless he changed his name to Tex." She pointed to the license plate on the back of the car.

"All right, everybody, ready to go in?" asked Fred.

The gang gathered around the green door.

"You're sure there are no dragons in there?" asked Shaggy.

"Absolutely," Velma said. "There's nothing in there to be afraid of."

As the gang opened the door, a loud scream filled the air.

"AAAAAAAAAAAAAAHHHHHHHHH-HHHH!"

"Zoinks!" Shaggy cried. "Sounds like you spoke too soon, Velma!"

Chapter 2

Shaggy and Scooby tried to run away. Daphne and Velma held onto Shaggy's shirt while Fred kept a tight grip on Scooby's collar.

"Man, my feet are moving but the rest of me's staying put!" Shaggy noticed.

"Me, roo!" Scooby said.

"That's because we're not letting you two run away," Velma said. "Now just take it easy. I'm sure there's a perfectly good explanation for what we just heard."

Shaggy and Scooby followed the others into the building. Just up ahead, they saw a man looking at his clipboard.

"Excuse me, but we're —" Fred began.

"Aaahh!" the man cried as he jumped back. He dropped his clipboard and his hat flew back off his head.

"We are so sorry," Daphne said, running over. "We didn't mean to startle you. It's just that we heard a scream and —"

The man nodded. "I know, I know, you thought maybe something happened to Wings," he said as he put his hat back on. A picture of Fireball the Dragon sat just above the brim.

"Hey, you're Coach Nelvin!" Fred said.

"That's right, son," Coach Nelvin replied. "And who are you?"

"I'm Fred, and this is Daphne, Velma, Shaggy, and Scooby-Doo," Fred said. "We won those passes the team donated to the charity bazaar last month."

9

Coach Nelvin slowly nodded. "Ah, so you're here for the all-access, behind-the-scenes look at the Dragons' brand-new practice facility," he said.

"Nelly, this isn't just any ol' brand-new practice facility," a voice thundered from down the hall.

The gang listened as a man thumped his way down the hall. A peculiar clicking sound accompanied his footsteps. The gang was puzzled until the man stepped from the shadows holding a cane.

"This is a world-class, multimillion-dollar practice facility!" the man continued. Though he was now much closer to Coach Nelvin and the gang, his voice still thundered out of him.

"Tex, please forgive me," Coach Nelvin said with a drop of weariness in his voice. "But I'm so busy trying to whip this team into shape that I forget to give this place its due."

"Don't worry about it, Nelly," the man said. "You don't work for me anymore . . . yet."

"Ruh?" asked Scooby.

"That goes double for me, pal," Shaggy whispered back.

"Tex Packemin's the name," the man said, extending his hand. "I used to own the Dragons. Even raised the money to build this place. Then my business went sour and I had to sell the team. But now I'm back on my feet. Or should I say, foot."

He raised up his right pant leg, revealing a bandage wrapped around his right ankle. "I was shootin' some hoops with the fellas and

11

ended up twisting my ankle a bit. But no worries. It'll be right as rain, just like things around here will be as soon as I figure out a way to get back control of the team. See ya, Nelly!"

Tex Packemin sauntered away, whistling and swinging his cane. He left through the green door.

"It's not going to be as easy as he thinks," Coach Nelvin sighed.

"But you've got Wings Monroe," Fred said.

"Wings Monroe is great, but he's only one player," Coach Nelvin said. "And if I don't figure out a way for us to win this year, there's no telling what the new owner will do."

"Like, maybe he can start by taking care of that bloodcurdling scream we heard," Shaggy suggested.

"Oh, that," Coach Nelvin said, managing a slight smile. "That came from the training room. Just someone working out with Rue Bernard, the cheerleaders' physical trainer."

"Jeepers, sounds like she's a pretty tough trainer," Daphne said.

"You don't know the half of it," Coach Nelvin said. "You know the expression 'no pain, no gain'? She's got one of her own: 'No screams, no dreams.'"

"Sounds like someone we should avoid, eh, Scoob?" Shaggy said.

"Roo bet!" Scooby agreed.

"Too late!" came a woman's voice from behind them.

Chapter 3

Startled, Shaggy and Scooby tried to jump into each other's arms. Instead, they crashed into each other and fell to the floor in a heap.

A tall, athletic-looking woman wearing a Dragons warm-up suit stepped forward. She looked at Shaggy and Scooby and shook her head sadly.

"Pathetic," she said. "If I had one hour with you two, you'd be doing flips into each other's arms like nobody's business. And you'd lose some of that excess baggage, too." She gave Scooby's flank a light tap with her foot.

"Take it easy, Rue," Coach Nelvin said.

"These kids are our guests today. They're here for a tour of the practice facility and to see the team warm up for tonight's preseason opener."

Rue Bernard's eyes lit up.

"A tour?" she asked. "There's no better place to start than the training room. Follow me." She helped Shaggy and Scooby up with a firm yank and started back down the hall. A bulky utility belt around Rue's waist clunked against her body as she walked.

"What is she wearing around her waist?" Daphne whispered to Coach Nelvin.

"It's a trainer's belt she devised," explained the coach. "It's got everything she needs in case a cheerleader gets injured: adhesive bandages, instant hot and cold packs, splints, aspirin, things like that."

"I never realized cheerleaders had it so rough," Fred said.

"One more thing," Coach Nelvin added. "She's a little sensitive about being the cheerleaders' trainer. She really wanted to be the basketball team's head trainer. But part of the deal that brought Wings to our team included making his trainer our team's head trainer."

"Let's go, people!" Rue shouted.

Shaggy and Scooby sprang to attention and sprinted down the hall. Fred, Daphne, and Velma thanked Coach Nelvin and followed. By the time they stepped into the training room, Rue Bernard had Shaggy and Scooby exercising.

Shaggy was sitting in the crunch machine. The device automatically folded him in half every five seconds to strengthen his stomach muscles.

"Golly, Shaggy, I didn't know you had it in you," Daphne called.

"All I know is that if this machine doesn't stop, it'll be all over me . . . along with my lunch," Shaggy moaned.

Scooby meanwhile was lying facedown

on a table. There
was a hole cut
in the table
for his face to
poke through.

"Now
this won't
hurt a bit."
Rue Bernard
smiled. She
stood over him
and slapped her hand against his back.

"Rikes!" whimpered Scooby.

"Just relax," Rue said as she began kneading the muscles in Scooby's back. Her gentle kneading soon turned into pounding and stretching.

Shaggy climbed out of the crunch machine and his body automatically folded itself in half. "Man, this is crazy," he said. "Look at me, Scoob. I'm a capital A."

17

Scooby giggled and, as Rue turned away, he managed to slither off the table. He tried to stand up, but his muscles were so relaxed he fell to the floor like a lump.

"Look at you, Scooby," Shaggy said. "You look like a pile of mashed potatoes. With gravy."

Fred looked at his watch. "I think we should be getting over to the gym," he said. "The team's starting their warm-ups now."

Rue heard this and frowned. "But what about the rest of your workout?" she called to Shaggy and Scooby-Doo. "We have to finish getting you into shape!"

"Like, no thanks," Shaggy called back. "We like our old shapes better!"

GOODLAND PUBLIC LIBRARY
GOODLAND, KANSAS 67735

Chapter 4

The gang walked through a set of double doors and into a large gymnasium. One side of the gym was lined with wooden bleachers. A mesh net hung down the center, dividing the gym in two. On one side, the cheerleaders were rehearsing one of their dance routines. On the other side, some of the Dragons were warming up. A few of the teammates stood in a circle, passing the ball between them without looking.

"Look, there's Studs Larkin," Fred said. He pointed to a player dribbling the ball up and down the court. "And there's Lenny Warble!"

Off to one side, Velma noticed another player trying to spin a basketball on his fingertip. "Who's that, Fred?" she asked.

Fred looked over. "Beats me," he shrugged.

"Whoever he is, he doesn't look very good," Daphne said. "I'll bet that bandage wrapped around his wrist doesn't help, either."

The ball spun off his finger and onto the floor. The player dove after it and tried to grab the ball and stand up at the same time.

"Ouch!" Shaggy said as the player toppled over. The ball rolled over to the gang. Fred picked it up and passed it to the player.

"Thanks," the player said.

"Excuse me, but I don't recognize you," Fred said. "Were you just traded to the team?"

"Not exactly," the player said. "I'm Chunk Torpor. I came over in the Wings Monroe trade. They cut me from the team yesterday."

"Oh, sorry," Fred said.

"Not your fault," Chunk replied. "The only person I blame is him." He pointed to Wings Monroe, who was joking around with some of the other players. "He's had it in for me since we started playing to-gether four years ago. I think he told Coach Nelvin that I wasn't a team player."

"That's terrible," Daphne said. "I can't believe

someone like Wings Monroe would do that to a teammate."

Coach Nelvin came out of the equipment room in time to overhear the conversation.

"Wings didn't have anything to do with it," the coach said. "It was my call."

"Yeah, yeah." Chunk nodded. "I know who really runs this team: the superstar player."

Coach Nelvin's expression soured. "I cut you yesterday, Torpor, so I don't even know how you snuck in here today," he said. "Now get out, before I call security."

"Fine with me, Nelly," he teased. Torpor turned and heaved the basketball through the air. Everyone watched as it arched up and headed toward the basket on the far side of the gym. The ball came down about six feet short of the backboard and bounced into the seats.

"Good-bye, Torpor," Coach Nelvin said.

Torpor spun around and stormed out through the gym's double doors. "Sorry you had to see that, kids. Now how about seeing some real basketball?"

The coach blew his whistle and the team ran over.

"Okay, guys, how about a little practice game for our guests here?" he asked.

The players nodded and ran back onto the floor. Before they started, Coach Nelvin walked over to the wall and flipped a switch. A loud humming sound filled the gym.

"Golly, there go the bleachers!" Daphne said. Sure enough, the bleacher seats began retracting into themselves. Soon, there was nothing left but a solid wooden wall.

"Play ball!" Coach Nelvin shouted.

Chapter 5

The gang watched in awe as the Dragons took to the floor. Half the team aligned themselves into the Dragons' famous "double wing" defense. The other half, led by Wings Monroe, charged down the court.

"Here's how Wings Monroe earned his name," Fred said. Wings started running toward the basket. Studs Larkin passed the ball to him. Wings leaped up, snatched the ball out of the air, and sailed up to the basket. He slammed the ball through the hoop and dropped to the ground.

"Zoinks!" Shaggy gasped. "He was flying! Did you see that, Scoob? The man was actually flying!"

Coach Nelvin smiled. "Atta boy, Wings!" he cheered over the players' high fives.

A moment later, a different sound filled the gym.

"What's that?" wondered Daphne.

"Probably someone else stuck in Rue Bernard's training room of torture," Shaggy joked.

The sound got louder and exploded into a deafening roar. The double doors flew open as some kind of monster ran into the gym.

"AAAAWWWWRRRROOOOAAAAR-RRR!" it howled. It ran to the middle of the gym and yanked open the dividing net.

"Jinkies!" Velma exclaimed. "What is that?"

The monster was unlike any creature they had ever seen. It had a wolf's fierce head, the imposing body of a bear, and sharp claws like

a jackal. The creature raced around the gym, herding the players, cheerleaders, and everyone else into the far corner.

"What do you think he wants?" Daphne asked.

"I'll tell you what I want!" the monster growled. "I want to fly like an eagle. And the only things I'm missing are wings!" At that, the horrible creature reached out and grabbed Wings Monroe.

"Hey! Keep your gross animal claws to your smelly self!" Wings protested. The monster grabbed Wings tighter and flipped him over his shoulder. Wings struggled, but he couldn't break free.

"Now let's see how you do without your star!" the monster taunted. "Let's see the mighty Dragons claw their way through the season!" As the monster ran back across the gym, Studs Larkin stepped forward.

"Let's get him!" he called. The other players rallied behind Studs and took off after the creature. The monster ran into the equipment room and locked the door behind him. When the players got there, they tried to break down the door but couldn't.

28

"There's another door through the training room!" Coach Nelvin cried. Studs ran out the main doors to the training room. When he returned a moment later, he wasn't smiling.

"It looks like he got away," Studs said. "With Wings."

"And our season," Coach Nelvin moaned. "I hate to say it, fellas, but without Wings, we're cooked. I guess I should go tell the owner."

Fred, Daphne, and Velma looked at one another and nodded.

"Hold on, Coach," Fred said. "We may not

know a lot about basketball, but we do know a thing or two about solving mysteries."

"That's awfully nice, kids, but I really don't think —" the coach began.

"Just give us one hour, Coach," Velma said. "We haven't lost a case yet, and I have a hunch the solution to this mystery is a lot closer than we think."

"What makes you say that?" asked Coach Nelvin.

Velma pointed to something stuck in the doorjamb to the equipment room. Everyone gathered around to get a closer look.

"Looks like a piece of cloth of some kind," Daphne said.

Velma yanked it out of the doorjamb. "It's no ordinary piece of cloth," she said, holding it out. Fred, Velma, Shaggy, and Scooby touched it.

"Eeewww," Scooby said.

"Sticky," Shaggy said.

"Just like an adhesive sports bandage," Velma clarified.

"Did Wings Monroe have any kind of injuries, Coach?" he asked.

"Nope, not yet," the coach answered.

Fred nodded along with Daphne and Velma. "All right, gang. It's time to get to work."

Chapter 6

Fred suggested that, in order to work fast, they split up.

"Daphne, you look around the gym with me while Velma, Shaggy, and Scooby check out the training room," he said.

Just as Fred turned to go, Velma cleared her throat. "I have a better idea, Fred," she said. "I say we all cover the gym now. It's a big room, and the five of us can do it in no time. Then Daphne and I can check out the cheerleaders' locker room while you look around the players' locker room."

"Like, what about us?" asked Shaggy.

"You two can go to the training room," Daphne said.

"Ruh-roh," Scooby said. "Rere we go ragain!" He fell to the floor like he did after Rue Bernard's fierce massage.

"Don't worry, Scooby, I'll protect you," Shaggy said. "Until the queen of pain shows up, that is. Then you're on your own."

"Let's not waste any more time chitchatting," Daphne said.

The gang quickly and efficiently walked around the entire gymnasium looking for clues. When it was clear there was nothing to be found, Fred, Daphne, and Velma headed to the locker rooms.

"I guess we'd better go and face the music, pal," Shaggy said. He led Scooby out of the gym and down the hall to the training room. They carefully peeked through the doorway to see if the coast was clear.

"Do you see anything, Scooby?" Shaggy whispered. "Look carefully."

Scooby squinted his eyes to squeeze every bit of careful looking out of them.

"Ruh-uh," Scooby answered.

Shaggy and Scooby slowly tiptoed into the room.

"It's awfully quiet in here," Shaggy whispered. "And you know what that means."

"Reeping rabies?" Scooby asked.

"No, Scoob, not sleeping babies!" Shaggy said. "It means that something bad's gonna happen. Man, I'm so scared, even my goose bumps have goose bumps."

Shaggy and Scooby heard something from the hallway. They spun around and backed the rest of the way into the room.

"Keep your ears peeled, pal," Shaggy said. "I don't want any creepy, growly, basketball-star-stealing monsters sneaking up on us."

They heard a strange sound, like a muffled scream, coming from somewhere in the room. Then they felt their backs bump up against something tall and hairy.

Shaggy reached his hand back to feel what it was.

"Uh, Scooby," Shaggy said shakily. "Like, tell me it's been a while since you had a haircut."

Scooby looked sideways at Shaggy and slowly shook his head.

"Rorry, Raggy," he whimpered.

Shaggy and Scooby slowly turned their heads and saw . . . the monster!

It snarled at them fiercely.

"Zoinks!" Shaggy cried.

"Rikes!" Scooby yelled.

"Let's get out of here!" Shaggy shouted. He and Scooby took off across the room. They ran harder and harder, trying to outpace the monster. Shaggy looked back.

"He's still on us, Scoob!" he shouted between gasps. "Run faster, Scooby!"

The two of them kept running, faster and faster. But no matter how fast they ran, the monster kept up. Shaggy glanced back over his shoulder and noticed that the monster was gone. "Hey, where'd it go?"

Shaggy looked forward again and came face-to-face with the creature.

"Man! What's going on here?" Shaggy cried. The creature pointed down at Shaggy's feet. Shaggy and Scooby looked down and discovered they were running on a treadmill.

"Man, no wonder this room seemed so long," Shaggy said.

The creature reached out and pushed a button on the treadmill's control panel. The belt sped up, making Shaggy and Scooby run faster and faster.

"I . . . can't . . . take . . . much . . . more . . . of . . . this!" Shaggy cried between gasps of air. He and Scooby stopped running and were instantly thrown off the treadmill. They flew backwards and crashed into a giant towel hamper.

"Quick, Scooby!" Shaggy cried. "Hide!"

GOODLAND PUBLIC LIBRARY
GOODLAND. KANSAS 67735

Chapter 7

Shaggy and Scooby burrowed beneath the towels, but it was no use. Someone was pulling the towels off faster than Shaggy and Scooby could dig. The last layer of towels finally flew off them.

"Please, don't hurt us, Mr. Monster!" Shaggy pleaded.

"What are you talking about, Shaggy?" asked Daphne.

"Ruh?" Scooby said, opening his eyes.

"What are you two doing in the towel hamper?" Velma asked.

"That monster chased us in here," Shaggy explained as he and Scooby climbed out.

Daphne and Velma took a look around the training room.

"Well, there's no one here now but us," Daphne said.

"And this," Velma added, noticing something on the floor by the treadmill. She reached down and picked up a small card. "It's an

entry permit just like ours. And it has today's date on it."

"Let's go see if we can find Fred and show him this clue," Daphne said.

Shaggy and Scooby followed Daphne and Velma back to the gym. Fred was already there, shooting baskets.

"Nice to see you hard at work, Fred," Velma said.

Fred spun around and smiled sheepishly. "Just, uh, taking a little break," he admitted. "Did you find anything?"

Velma showed him the parking permit. Fred smiled.

"I'm glad you found something," he said. "Because I didn't find anything in the locker room."

"I'm afraid we're running out of time," Daphne added.

"What about us?" asked Shaggy. "Like, don't you care that we were almost eaten alive by that thing?"

"You're right, Shaggy," Velma said. "If you weren't almost eaten alive, we never would have found the clue. Good work."

Shaggy turned to say something to Scooby, but Scooby wasn't there. Shaggy heard the sound of a bouncing basketball. He looked up and saw Scooby dribbling the ball down the court. Scooby tossed the ball up into the air.

Shaggy followed the ball as it rose up into the air and then started falling. "Heads up, Scoob!" Shaggy called.

Scooby stopped and looked over at Shaggy. "Ruh?" he asked.

41

The ball came down on Scooby's head and bounced off with a dull *THUD*!

"Rouch!" Scooby cried, rubbing his head. The others ran over to see if he was all right.

"You okay, pal?" asked Shaggy.

Before Scooby could answer, a basketball came hurtling from above. It hit the floor right next to Fred and bounced away. Then another fell and bounced away. And another. And another. Pretty soon, a whole mess of basketballs was flying through the air at the gang.

"Jinkies!" Velma cried. "It's raining basketballs!"

"Courtesy of our friendly neighborhood monster!" Daphne said.

The monster stood perched atop the bleachers, now open again. He tossed basketballs down at the gang.

"Quick, let's take cover!" Fred shouted. "Follow me!"

The gang ran across the gym with their

arms over their heads to protect themselves from the basketballs. The monster climbed down the bleachers and chased after the gang. It growled and snarled all the way.

Fred found the door to the equipment room unlocked.

"In here!" he instructed.

Everyone ran into the equipment room and ducked behind a rack of basketballs. They heard a *CLICK* and realized only too late what had just happened.

"That monster tricked us into running in here," Daphne said.

"He locked the door and trapped us like animals," Velma agreed.

"Speaking of animals, it looks like a few of them exploded back here," Shaggy said. He pointed to a pile of animal costumes including a bear, a wolf, an eagle, and a jackal.

"These must be left over from the mascot contest the team had a while back," Fred

said. "Now we know where our creature's unique appearance comes from."

"A lot of good that does us when we're locked in here," Shaggy said.

"As a matter of fact, Shaggy, being locked in here is just what we needed to figure out this mystery," Velma said.

Shaggy and Scooby looked at Velma like she was crazy.

"Velma's right," Fred agreed. "And now that we know who's behind it, it's time to set a trap."

chapter 8

Fred gathered everyone around and explained his plan.

"First, Velma and I are going to rerig the net dividing the gym," he said. "Once that's done, we'll have Coach Nelvin start another team practice as usual. And that's where you come in." He looked right at Shaggy and Scooby, who were busy trying on the different parts of the mascot costumes.

"Rho, me?" Scooby asked. He looked up, wearing the eagle's head.

"Scooby, take that off and pay attention," Velma said.

"We'll ask Coach Nelvin for a couple of practice jerseys," Fred said. "You two will be out on the floor with the rest of the team. When the monster shows up, you'll need to get him to chase you up the bleachers."

"That's it?" asked Shaggy.

Fred nodded. "Then Daphne will hit the switch to close up the bleachers again," Fred added. "You two will jump down onto the cheerleaders' trampoline. And we'll drop the divider net on him."

"Great plan, Freddie," Daphne said.

"Except for one teeny, tiny part," Shaggy said.

"Which part?" asked Velma.

"The teeny, tiny part where Scooby and I get chased by the hairy horror!" Shaggy replied.

"But you get to play basketball with the Dragons!" Fred said.

Shaggy and Scooby folded their arms and turned their backs on the others.

"You get to wear the cool practice jerseys!" Daphne said.

"You get a Scooby Snack!" Velma offered.

Scooby's eyes lit up. "Roh, boy!" he cheered. Daphne tossed the snack over to Scooby, who gobbled it up and rubbed his stomach.

"Aaaaahhhh," he said with a broad smile. "Ret's play rall!" he barked.

The gang heard a click. They turned and watched the door slowly open. Shaggy and Scooby ducked down behind Fred, Daphne, and Velma.

"Anyone in here?" called Coach Nelvin.

"Just the man we're looking for," Fred said. "Coach, we need your help to catch the monster and save Wings."

Fred explained the plan. Coach Nelvin quickly agreed and went to get the rest of the team. Fred and Velma took care of the divider net, and Daphne took her position next to the control switch for the bleachers.

The players returned. Coach Nelvin rolled a rack of basketballs out of the equipment room. He blew his whistle to start the practice. As the players got into position, Shaggy and Scooby tried to figure out where to go.

"Heads up!" Studs Larkin called. He passed the ball to Shaggy. The ball slammed into Shaggy's chest, sending him staggering backwards.

"Sorry, man." Studs laughed as he ran down the court. Scooby-Doo managed to keep up with him and the other players. He found himself under the basket when someone passed the ball to him. Scooby jumped up and scored.

"Way to go, Scoob!" Shaggy cheered.

"Way to go!" echoed a fierce-sounding voice. Shaggy turned and saw the basketball monster standing behind him.

"Zoinks! It's him!" cried Shaggy.

The monster roared and started after

Shaggy. The other players backed off the court, leaving Shaggy and Scooby alone with the monster. According to plan, Shaggy and Scooby ran straight for the bleachers. They jogged up with the monster close behind.

The monster heard a humming sound and stopped.

"Time to abandon ship, Scoob!" Shaggy gasped. He and Scooby ran to the edge of the seats and jumped off. But before Velma and Fred could drop the net, the monster ran to the edge and jumped off after them.

Shaggy bounced off the trampoline and

rolled onto the cheerleaders' gymnastics mats. Scooby hit the trampoline and bounced back into the air. He came down on the basketball rack.

"Rouch!" Scooby barked.

As the monster ran toward Scooby, the whole rack of balls rolled toward him. The creature couldn't get out of the way and found himself tripping over the balls. He landed with a thud on the hardwood floor.

"Now, Velma!" Fred called. They gave the divider net a yank, guiding it over the monster as it fell. The monster was caught!

Chapter 9

Coach Nelvin ran over to Fred, Velma, and the trapped monster.

"You did it! You did it!" he cheered.

"Now let's take a look at who's been behind all this mischief," Velma said. She and Fred pulled the net off the monster's head. "Would you care to do the honors, Coach?" She motioned toward the creature's wolflike head.

Coach Nelvin reached over and grabbed the head. He gave it a tug and the mask came off in his hand.

"Rue Bernard!" gasped Coach Nelvin. "You did all this?"

"Just as we suspected," Daphne said.

"How did you kids figure it out?" asked the coach.

"Well, it wasn't easy," Daphne continued.

She explained that it took some careful detective work to connect the clues they found to their suspects.

"Clues? Like what?" Coach Nelvin wondered.

"Like the piece of adhesive bandage we found stuck to the door of the equipment room, remember?" Fred said. "That clue connected three different people to the mystery. And each of them had a motive, too, so they became our suspects."

"Chunk Torpor wore a bandage on his

wrist, and he was angry about being cut from the team," Velma said. "Rue Bernard had her trainer's belt with bandages, and she was unhappy about not getting the head trainer's job."

"And then there's Tex Packemin, who hurt his ankle playing basketball," Daphne added. "He seemed to have his heart set on getting the team back, no matter what the cost."

Coach Nelvin looked a little puzzled. "But with three suspects, how did you narrow it down?" he asked.

"That's where Shaggy and Scooby came in," Velma said. She explained how the monster chased after them in the training room. And when it did, it left something behind: an entry pass with today's date on it.

"So that means the monster needed a pass to get in," Daphne said.

"So?" The coach shrugged.

"So, of the three suspects, only two of

them would have a pass," Fred said. "Mr. Packemin and Rue Bernard."

Coach Nelvin still wasn't sure why. Fred cleared things up when he reminded the coach that Chunk Torpor wasn't supposed to be in the building today. He had snuck inside to hang out at practice. So he'd be the only one without a pass. That meant he couldn't be the monster.

"But that still left two suspects," Daphne said. "Until we got locked into the equipment room."

Shaggy stepped forward. "By the way, Coach," he said. "You know

you've got some animal parts in there, right? Very freaky, man."

Coach Nelvin smiled. "Yeah, left over from the mascot tryouts a few years back." Then he turned back to the others. "So how did getting locked inside the equipment room help you?"

"Whoever locked us in needed a key to the room," Velma said. "And of the two suspects, only one of them worked here and would have a key."

"Especially because one set of the doors led to the training room," Daphne added.

Coach Nelvin's eyes lit up. "Oh, so it had to be Rue!" he announced. He looked over at the trainer. "But why?"

Rue's mouth turned into a frown. "Why? Because I deserved that job!" she answered. "And if I couldn't have it, this team was going to pay! I knew that if Wings were gone and the team did badly enough, you'd be fired, Nelvin. And then I'd have a chance to move up. And it was all going along perfectly. Until those annoying kids and their out-of-shape dog showed up."

"Speaking of Wings, where is he?" Coach Nelvin demanded.

"Take it easy, Coach," Studs Larkin called. "We got him!"

Studs and some other players walked into the gym with Wings Monroe. "He was locked in the towel closet in the training room," Studs said. "We heard some muffled shouts and got him out."

"Well, I'm glad this is over," Coach Nelvin said. "I'll give security a call. Fellas, keep an eye on Rue. And kids, how can I ever thank you?"

Scooby smiled and looked at Shaggy.

"Like, I think my pal here has an idea," he said.

That night, at the Dragons' first game of the season, Fred, Daphne, Velma, and Shaggy sat in the best courtside seats. The team was ahead when the halftime horn blew. The cheerleaders ran onto the floor and began their routine. Then, from the rear of the group, a new cheerleader bounded up and sprang off the trampoline. It was Scooby!

He flipped into the air and landed on top of the cheerleaders' human pyramid. The fans roared with excitement as Fred, Daphne, Velma, and Shaggy laughed.

"Scooby-Dooby-Doo!" cheered Scooby.

About the Author

JF
Gelsey, James
Scooby-Doo! and the Hoopster
  Horror

As a boy, James Gelsey used to run home from school to watch the Scooby-Doo cartoons on television (only after finishing his homework). Today, he still enjoys watching them with his wife and two daughters. He also has a real dog named Scooby who loves nothing more than a good Scooby Snack!

GOODLAND PUBLIC LIBRARY
GOODLAND, KANSAS 67735